Little Pear and His Friends

Also by Eleanor Frances Lattimore

LITTLE PEAR

Little Pear and His Friends

ELEANOR FRANCES LATTIMORE

Illustrated by the author

AN ODYSSEY/HARCOURT YOUNG CLASSIC

HARCOURT, INC.

Orlando   Austin   New York   San Diego   Toronto   London

www.HarcourtBooks.com

First Harcourt Young Classics edition 2005
First Odyssey Classics edition 1991
First published 1934

Library of Congress Cataloging-in-Publication Data
Lattimore, Eleanor Frances, 1904–1986
Little Pear and his friends/Eleanor Frances Lattimore; illustrated by the author.
p.   cm.
"An Odyssey Classic."
Summary: Six-year-old Little Pear has many adventures with Big Head and
his other friends in his village in China.
[1. China—Fiction.]   I. Title.
PZ7.L37Ld   2005
[Fic]—dc22   2004059659
ISBN-13: 978-0152-05484-7   ISBN-10: 0-15-205484-7
ISBN-13: 978-0152-05490-8 (pb)   ISBN-10: 0-15-205490-1 (pb)

Text set in Bodoni

A C E G H F D B
A C E G H F D B (pb)

Printed in the United States of America

CONTENTS

Little Pear and His Friends

1

A Surprise for Little Pear

There is a village in China called Shegu. All around it are flat fields where the farmers make vegetables grow, and far away on one side is a great highway, and far away on the other side is a river. The highway leads to a city, and the river leads to the sea.

In this village there once lived a boy called Little

Pear. His head was shaved except for one spot of hair above his forehead that was tied up in a little pigtail. His eyes were like black apple-seeds, and although his round face looked solemn, the little pigtail that stood straight up in the air looked rather mischievous.

Little Pear's family was very fond of him, but they often thought that he was naughty. This was because he always liked to be doing something, and the things he did often seemed to lead to trouble. Once he burnt a hole in his new jacket when he lit a firecracker and forgot to stand back, and once he ate three green peaches and felt very sick indeed. Another time he fell into the river.

"Don't get into mischief, Little Pear," his mother used to say to him, and his father used to say, "You mustn't run away." It was hard for Little Pear to remember all the things he was not supposed to do.

Little Pear was six years old. He was the youngest in his family. His big sister, Dagu, was eleven years old, and his second sister, Ergu, was eight years old. They were good little girls and never had to be scolded about anything. Dagu helped her mother about the house and sewed, and Ergu ran errands and sometimes sewed, too. Dagu's hair was braided into one long braid and Ergu's was braided into two shorter ones. They both wore tiny gold earrings.

Little Pear kept wishing that he was not the youngest in his family. Being the youngest meant that all the rest of the family were always trying to take care of him.

"Ay-ah!" thought Little Pear. "I wish I had a little brother! If I had a little brother I could take care of *him*. Then everyone would know that I was a big boy."

The house that Little Pear and his family lived in was made of sun-baked bricks the color of dust. There was only one room in it, and nearly half the room was filled by a huge gray brick bed. On top of the bed was a straw mat and on top of that there were quilts which were spread out at night and rolled up during the day. The family all slept on the bed and ate their meals there too, gathered around a small short-legged table.

There were three windows in the house, with many little panes in them made of paper instead of glass. And there was one door, which led into the courtyard in front of the house.

The courtyard had a high wall all around it. It was so high that you could see nothing over the top of it except sky and clouds. But in the wall there was a gateway leading to the street. And if you stood in the gateway you could see quite a bit of the world, because the house was at the end of the street and at the edge of the village.

Little Pear loved to stand in the gateway looking across the fields. Far away was the river. He couldn't see the river but he could see the row of willow trees along the bank and sometimes tall brown sails moving slowly behind them.

There were two stone lions in front of the gateway, one on either side of the door. They looked as though they were guarding it, like two watchdogs. They had curly manes and round staring eyes, and

The house that Little Pear lived in

their mouths were wide open. But they couldn't bite. Little Pear was not at all afraid of them.

One day Little Pear stood in the gateway, balancing on the high wooden step. He had been playing with his friends in the village all day and now it was time for him to go home to his afternoon meal. Little Pear felt rather hungry, but he didn't want to go into the house just yet. He was looking towards the river where the boats were, and wishing that he could go there again and not fall in this time.

He was thinking, "I wish I could be big right away. Then I would have a great ship of my own and I would sail down the river to the sea." While he was thinking he heard somebody call, "Little Pear! Little Pear!" It sounded like his sister Ergu.

"I'm coming!" Little Pear called back; but he stood right where he was a minute longer.

"Little Pear!" called Ergu again, and she came running out of the house and across the courtyard. "Come quickly, Little Pear," she said. "There is something in our house that you have never seen before."

Ergu looked excited and Little Pear suddenly felt excited, too. He wondered what there could be in the house that he had never seen before.

"Is it a toy?" he asked. "Or is it something to eat?"

Little Pear stood in the gateway

Ergu wouldn't tell. "Come and see," she said. "It's a surprise."

So Little Pear followed Ergu into the house. He looked all around the room. There was his sister Dagu in front of the stove, preparing the meal. And there was his father, looking very pleased. And there on the wide brick bed was his mother, holding something small wrapped up in a quilt.

"Is that it?" asked Little Pear. But before Ergu

could say, "Yes," his mother said, "Come and look, Little Pear. This is your little brother."

Little Pear went up to the bed and peeked inside the quilt. His brother was very small. He was smaller than the little brothers or sisters of any of his friends. He was so small that he made Little Pear feel enormous. He had never felt so big in all his life before. It was a good feeling not to be the youngest anymore, and to have a brother.

"I can take care of him!" said Little Pear.

2

Big Head's Good Idea

When the new brother was one month old he was
given a name. He was called Shing-er. All the people
in the village came to see him then, and they brought
him many presents—jackets and trousers made of
satin, and embroidered caps and shoes. They brought
him toys, too, and strings of money. It was important
to be one month old, and to have a name.

Little Pear's best friend came to see Shing-er with the others. He brought him a toy, a cloth tiger with green glass eyes. Little Pear's best friend was called Big Head. He was a little older than Little Pear, and his face was even more solemn, but he was almost as mischievous as Little Pear.

Big Head had a brother too, but his brother was three years old instead of one month old and nobody was bringing him any presents. He had a name but nobody ever remembered it because he was always just called "Didi," which means "little brother."

As soon as Big Head saw Shing-er, he said, "I have a brother, too."

"A new one?" asked Little Pear in great surprise.

"No," said Big Head. "He is three years old."

"Oh, I've seen that brother lots of times," said Little Pear.

Big Head was silent a minute and then he said, "A brother three years old is better than one who is only one month old. He can walk and talk."

Little Pear began to feel rather sad. It was nice to have a brother that everybody was bringing presents to—but he wished that his brother could walk and talk.

One day some time later his mother said to him, "Shing-er is asleep, and I am going out now to do the marketing. Will you help your sisters to mind your brother while I am gone, Little Pear?"

"Yes," said Little Pear. "I will hold him and be very careful not to drop him."

So Little Pear held the baby, while Dagu and Ergu stitched away, making clothes for him. Ergu was making a little coat, and Dagu was embroidering a pair of shoes with bats' wings on the toes, for good luck. In the birdcage that hung against the wall above them their pet bird hopped about and sang.

The day was warm, so the door of the house was kept open. Little Pear sat on the doorstep with Shinger, who was fast asleep. He was nearly two months old now but he couldn't walk or talk yet.

Little Pear sat so still that soon his legs felt tired. His arms were tired, too, from holding Shing-er. It was harder work taking care of him than he had thought it would be. He got up from the doorstep and walked across the courtyard, taking care all the time not to drop Shing-er.

"Don't go away," said Dagu.

"I won't," said Little Pear. But he went as far as the gateway. Shing-er opened his eyes, but before he could start to cry Little Pear held him up so that he could see the trees by the river.

"There is the river," said Little Pear. "You must never, never fall into it."

Just then Big Head came walking along the street. He was taking care of his little brother, too. His

brother was walking by his side and talking. They both stopped to speak to Little Pear and to look at Shing-er.

Didi's head was shaved except for a fringe across his forehead. He wore a pink jacket with blue flowers on it, and red trousers. He looked very fine, but so did Shing-er who was all dressed up in some of his new clothes.

"I have a good idea," said Big Head to Little Pear. "Let's exchange our brothers! I will take Shing-er home to my house and you may keep Didi here with you. Our mothers will be very much surprised!"

Big Head's idea was so sudden that Little Pear

hardly had time to think. Before he knew it he had handed Shing-er over to Big Head. Shing-er had gone to sleep again so he didn't know he was being exchanged, and Didi was so astonished that he said nothing at all. He sat down on the step between the two stone lions and Little Pear sat down beside him.

They watched Big Head carrying Shing-er off down the street.

Little Pear felt rather worried as he watched them disappear around the corner, but he felt pleased, too.

For now he had a brother who could walk and talk.

Meanwhile Ergu had grown tired of sewing. She usually got tired of it before Dagu did.

"Little Pear," she called. "I will take care of the baby now. You can go and play."

But when Ergu came out of the house to fetch Shing-er he was nowhere to be seen! And there was Big Head's brother instead.

"You naughty boy!" said Ergu to Little Pear. "This is not ours!" And she pointed her finger at poor Didi, who began to cry.

"Don't let the baby cry!" called Dagu from inside the house; and she came running out to see what the trouble was. "You naughty boy!" she cried. "What have you done with Shing-er?"

Dagu ran off, with Ergu at her heels

Dagu was holding the baby

Little Pear looked down at his shoes. He felt sorry now that he and Big Head had exchanged their brothers, because he knew it had been a mistake.

"Big Head has taken Shing-er home with him," he said. "We have his brother instead."

Dagu didn't wait to hear any more but ran off toward Big Head's house with Ergu at her heels. Little Pear followed more slowly, leading Didi by the hand. He was feeling more worried all the time. What if Big Head wouldn't give Shing-er back to them? But on their way they met Big Head, coming toward them. He was still carrying Shing-er.

"My mother wants Didi back again," he said. "You may have Shing-er!"

So Dagu took Shing-er and Big Head took his own brother. And by the time Little Pear's mother came home from the market her family was just as she had left them, except that now it was Dagu who was holding the baby, while Little Pear fed the bird. So she was not surprised after all.

But Little Pear never wanted to exchange his brother for anybody else's again—even if he couldn't walk and talk!

3

How Little Pear Helped His Sisters
Gather Leaves

In the fall, when the wind began to blow the leaves off the trees, the children of the village were sent out to gather them up from the ground. They brought them home to their families, for the dry leaves made good fires in the stoves and kept the houses warm.

One day in the fall Dagu and Ergu left the village and started off across the fields toward the highroad.

They were going to gather the leaves that had fallen from the trees there. They had baskets on their backs, fastened over their shoulders with straps. In their hands they carried long rakes made of bamboo. The rakes were to rake up the leaves with, and the baskets were to put the leaves in.

Dagu and Ergu each had on an extra coat because the day was cold. The wind blew in their faces and made their cheeks red. They started out chattering gaily to each other. They thought it was fun to leave their house and to go out and rake up leaves.

Little Pear stood in the gateway watching them go. He wanted to gather leaves too, but his mother said that he was too small. Little Pear felt sad, because he wanted to work like the others. He was tired of playing, and he couldn't take care of his brother all the time.

When his sisters had gone quite a long distance Little Pear suddenly felt that he couldn't stay behind a minute longer. He ran back into the house where his mother was rocking Shing-er to sleep.

"Mother," he said, "may I go with Dagu and Ergu this time? I am six years old now, and I'm not the youngest anymore. I want to gather leaves with the others!"

His mother looked doubtful. "I am afraid you may get lost or run away," she said.

"Oh, no!" said Little Pear. "I want to work now."

His mother smiled. "Very well," she said. "You may go. There is another rake, and here is a basket. See how many leaves you can gather!"

She put an extra jacket on Little Pear, and fastened the basket on his back. Little Pear took the rake and hurried off. Across the courtyard and over the high step of the gate he went; and then he ran down the path that led across the fields. His basket

bounced up and down against his back and his long rake went bump, bump, bump, behind him along the ground. "Wait for me, Dagu! Wait for me, Ergu!" cried Little Pear.

Dagu and Ergu were far ahead. They couldn't hear him calling them at first. They were walking, though, and Little Pear was running. He drew nearer and nearer to them and at last he was near enough for them to hear him. And then they stopped and waited.

Little Pear came panting up to them. He was rather fat and he was quite out of breath from running so fast. "Ay-ah!" he said. "That was hard work!"

Dagu and Ergu both began to laugh. "We haven't started working yet," they said.

They had reached the highroad now. It stretched like a long wall ahead of them, and they couldn't see over the top of it. A steep slope led up to the top of the highroad and along the slope two rows of

trees were planted, a row of peach trees and a row of willow trees. Their branches were bent by the wind and their leaves had fallen on the ground below them.

Little Pear thought that he had never seen so many leaves before. Surely there had never been so many on the trees as there were now on the ground. "Must we pick them all up?" he asked.

"Oh, no," said Dagu. "Only as many as our baskets will hold." And she showed Little Pear how to rake them up.

First, they took the baskets off their backs and set them on the ground. Then they raked the leaves into little piles, and then they tossed them into the baskets.

Little Pear had some trouble with his leaves. The wind kept blowing them away as soon as he had raked a few together, and they went in his face and down his neck! At last, however, he managed to get some into his basket before they blew away, and he was very proud then. He could rake leaves just like the others!

It was hard work, though. The long rake was heavy to handle, so after a while Little Pear laid it on the ground beside the basket, and sat down to rest. The dry leaves made a soft bed all around him. He lay down on his back to look at the clouds blow-

They raked the leaves into little piles

ing along in the windy sky. But the sky was so bright that he shut his eyes. Soon he was fast asleep.

"Look at Little Pear," said Dagu. "He is tired already."

"Let's not wake him up," said Ergu. "He ran so fast to catch up with us."

Then she had an idea. She put some more leaves into Little Pear's partly filled basket, and when Dagu saw her doing that she put some leaves in too. Soon Little Pear's basket was full and overflowing.

Then Dagu and Ergu wandered on, raking up leaves for their own baskets and talking to each other. And when they met some other children from the village who had also come to gather leaves, they joined them, and forgot all about their brother.

When Little Pear opened his eyes he was all

alone. At first he wondered where he was, and then he remembered and wondered where the others were instead. The village looked far away, but the high-road was very near. Little Pear wakened to the sound of cart wheels, and the klop, klop of horses' hoofs. He forgot that he had been gathering leaves, and scrambled up the steep slope to the highroad.

The highroad was the longest road in the world, Little Pear thought. It went on and on across the fields, and when it came to a village it turned into a street, but beyond the village it became a highroad again. Little Pear knew that at the end of the high-road was the city. He had been there once. And always along the highroad people were passing, in carts or in rickshaws or on foot, going to and from the city.

The carts had wheels higher than Little Pear's head. They had rounded tops made of blue cloth with windows in the sides for people to look out of. The drivers sat in the open fronts, swinging their legs and cracking long whips with red tassels on the ends of them.

Little Pear wished that he might go to the city again. But he had promised not to run away, and so he just stood by the side of the road and looked at everything. He looked at the carts and rickshaws going by. The men who pulled the rickshaws ran,

He stood by the side of the road

even though their loads were sometimes heavy. In one rickshaw there was a very old man with a long white beard, and in another there was a lady, with fine rich clothes and jeweled hands. The rickshaw pullers wore short coats tied in around their waists with sashes and long trousers tied around their ankles with strips of cloth. Their cloth-soled shoes went padding swiftly along the road.

But what interested Little Pear most of all were two little boys who were running beside the carts and rickshaws, holding out their hands. They were beggar boys, and their clothes were torn and patched. "Give us some money! Give us some money!" they were crying; and some of the people paid no attention to them, but others tossed pennies into their hands.

"I should like to be a beggar, too," thought Little Pear. "Think of all the money I could take home to my mother! We should soon be rich." But just then he remembered something. His mother had sent him to rake up leaves, and where were the leaves he had raked? What if someone had carried away his basket!

Little Pear slid and tumbled down the slope of the highroad in his hurry to find his basket and his rake. And as he did so he thought, "What a lazy boy I've been. I hardly gathered any leaves at all!"

But when he reached the bottom of the slope, there was the rake, and there was the basket just

where he had left them. And the basket was quite full and nearly overflowing with dry leaves.

"I must have raked up lots of leaves after all," thought Little Pear. And he hoisted his basket on his back and marched off happily toward home, trailing his rake, bump, bump, bump, behind him.

When he reached home he found his family all looking worried because he had not come home with the others. Dagu and Ergu had been scolded for the first time in their lives for forgetting all about him, and a scolding was waiting for Little Pear, too, for being so late.

But when his mother saw what a big basketful of leaves he had brought home she forgot to spank him and said, "Oh, Little Pear! How many leaves you have gathered!" and looked very pleased. Dagu

and Ergu looked at each other and laughed, and so Little Pear laughed too.

"It's fun raking leaves," he thought.

And that night there was a roaring fire in the stove that kept them all warm even though the wind was blowing outside.

4

How Little Pear Went Skating and Caught a Fish

It was winter now. Every leaf had blown off every tree and had been raked up. All the boys in the village went sliding every day on the pond that was just north of the village. Little Pear loved to slide, and he wished that Shing-er were big enough to slide, too. It couldn't be much fun being a baby, he thought, and not being able to slide or even walk. He felt very sorry for poor little Shing-er.

When Little Pear went out-of-doors now he wore two extra coats with padded linings and long sleeves that came clear down over his fingers to keep them warm. He also wore a cap with flaps at the sides to keep his ears warm. Dressed like this he was quite ready to run and slide.

One day Little Pear's father made him a skate, just like the kind the bigger boys had. It was made out of a flat piece of wood. Chinese boys use only one skate, because they slide on just one foot and push themselves along with the other.

Little Pear was very happy because he had a skate. He wanted to go out on the pond and skate right away. So he put on all his winter clothes and went out-of-doors, holding his skate tightly in one hand.

He hurried down the narrow village street, past gateways leading into other people's courtyards, and when he came to Big Head's house he stopped and shouted, "Big Head! Come and skate!" But Big Head didn't answer. He had probably gone out to the pond already.

Little Pear hurried on as fast as he could in his padded coats. He went past the shops with their open fronts; the food shops where hot food was set

"Big Head!" he shouted

out on tables, and the toy shop where all sorts of
toys were spread out on counters. But he went right
past the shops even though the food smelt good and
the toys looked exciting, because he was anxious to
get to the pond and begin skating.

When he got to the end of the village there was
an open field before him and in it was the pond, all
frozen over with thick ice. Little Pear ran down the
path to the pond and fastened on his skate. Big
Head was already skating, and so were the other
boys. "Look!" cried Little Pear. "I have a skate,
too!" Then he started himself off with a great push
and a long slide. But at the end of the slide he fell
down—ker-plunk!—because his skate went faster

than he did. He sat down for a minute feeling rather surprised, but he hardly felt the bump at all because of his padded coats.

He picked himself up and slid again and this time he didn't fall down. "It's quite easy skating, after all," thought Little Pear. And then he suddenly noticed that he had lost his skate! There it was behind him in the place where he had fallen. He hurried back to pick it up, but he didn't put it on again right away. Sliding without skates was more fun, he thought.

Some of the older boys on the pond were rather rude, though. "Get out of our way!" they kept shouting. "You are too small to take up so much room, and you are not really skating at all!"

Little Pear felt angry because he didn't like to be told that he was small. He put on his skate again in a hurry and started off once more, with a great shove—and this time he slid a long way and didn't fall down.

"I can skate as well as you can!" he shouted to the big boys.

But the pond was so crowded that even a good skater had a hard time steering. There were too many people to bump into. After Little Pear had bumped into about three other boys and had been bumped

into by about four he decided to go and skate some-
where else where there was more room. He imme-
diately thought of the river.

So he took off his skate and walked across the
field to the river.

The river was frozen over as hard as the pond.
Ice-sleds were skimming down it instead of boats,
but they kept to the middle of it and there was a
clear strip along the side where one or two people
were already skating.

Little Pear scrambled down the bank and fastened on his skate once more. And the wind blew
him along so fast that he couldn't stop himself.

"Look out!" he heard somebody say. "Don't fall into the hole!" And there right in front of him was a square hole cut in the ice, and a man squatting beside it, fishing. Little Pear sat down hard on the ice, just in time.

"If you had fallen in I should have had to catch you instead of a fish," laughed the man.

But all Little Pear said was, "May I watch you?"

"You may watch if you don't come too close," replied the fisherman.

The fisherman was very old. He had a gray beard and a kind wrinkled face. He was dressed in a warm coat lined with sheepskin, and he had straw boots on his feet to keep the cold out.

He fished with a long pole with a spike on the end; and while he fished he told Little Pear how he had cut the hole, and how deep under the ice there were fish lying in the mud of the river bottom. All the year round he fished, he said, but fishing in winter was harder than at any other time. It was hard work cutting holes in the ice, and cold work fishing.

Little Pear had forgotten all about skating now, he was so interested in fishing. He didn't mind sitting still even though he became so cold that his feet felt frozen to the ice. He was almost as pleased as the fisherman was when a small fish was finally caught and placed securely in a basket.

"I wish I could catch a fish, too," he thought. And all at once he thought of Shing-er who was too little to come out-of-doors and play.

"Please will you let me catch just one fish?" he asked the fisherman. "I only want to catch one fish, to take home to my little brother."

The fisherman was in a good humor because he had already caught twelve. So he said, "Very well, you may try. Hold the pole this way, and push it down till it touches the mud. If it hits something that feels like a fish, pull it up quickly."

So Little Pear did as he was told. He pushed the pole down, but when it touched the mud it seemed to stick there. He couldn't pull it up!

The fisherman took hold of the pole, too. "I will help you," he said. Together they pulled up the pole, and there on the. end was a fish! Little Pear had never felt so excited before in all his life.

"You are a very good fisherman," said the old man, as he took the fish off the spike and put it into a little extra basket that he had. "You caught a fish the first time! Hurry home with it now before you catch cold, and give it to your little brother."

Little Pear thanked the fisherman and took the basket. He held it tightly as he carefully climbed the bank and ran across the field to the village. His new skate was left behind because he had forgotten all about it.

Home ran Little Pear, and by the time he reached his house he was quite warm from running.

There in the house were all his family and something good was cooking on the stove.

"Time for supper, Little Pear," said his mother. "Did you have a good time skating?"

"Oh, yes," said Little Pear happily, and he held

Together they pulled up the pole

out the basket with both hands. Everybody was very much surprised to see the fish.

"Did someone give it to you, Little Pear?" asked his mother.

"No," said Little Pear. "I caught it myself, but a fisherman helped me. It is for Shing-er."

His mother laughed. "Shing-er is too small to eat fish yet," she said. "You had better eat it yourself. I will cook it for your supper."

Supper that night was delicious. Besides noodles with egg sauce, and tea, there was a crisp brown fish, the fish that Little Pear had caught for Shing-er. Little Pear had some, and so did Dagu, and so did Ergu, and so did their father and mother. But Shing-er lay on the bed and kicked his feet and didn't seem to mind at all that he was too small to have any.

5

How Little Pear Rode on an Ice-Sled, and Fell Off

Little Pear loved to stand on the riverbank, looking at the river. It was always different, and things were always happening there. All spring and summer and fall there were boats going up or down the river. Big boats and small boats, fishing boats and houseboats, boats with sails and rowboats: all the different kinds of boats you could possibly imagine.

In winter, though, there were ice-sleds instead of boats.

Little Pear had been in a boat once, but he had never been on an ice-sled. He wished that he might go for a ride on one sometime. They went so fast!

One day in the winter Little Pear's father had to go to the city on business. He could have gone in a cart or in a rickshaw or even on foot, although the city was a long way off. But he decided that the best way to go to the city would be by going down the river on an ice-sled.

Dagu, Ergu, and Little Pear all listened with great interest when they heard their father say he was going to the city on an ice-sled. They didn't ask to go, but they all looked rather sad.

"I've never been on an ice-sled," said Little Pear.

"We've never been to the city," said Dagu and Ergu.

Their father was good-natured, and so he said, "If you all three promise to be good children I will take you with me."

Of course Dagu, Ergu, and Little Pear all promised. They were so delighted at the idea of a ride down the river that they knew it wouldn't be hard to be good.

"May Shing-er come, too?" they asked, but their

Of course they all promised

mother said, "No, he is too little and he might catch cold. He must stay at home with me and keep me company."

It was a good day for a trip to the city. Although it was very cold there was no wind and the sun was shining. The three children put on their warmest clothes and went off with their father, across the field to the river, and their mother stood in the gateway with Shing-er and watched them go.

The river looked dark and shiny between its dust-colored banks. There were a few people skating near the edge, and there were two fishermen, but the middle of the river was for the ice-sleds. There was a long line of them going by. They were low and flat and their long runners stuck out behind them. Men stood on the runners, with long spiked poles in their hands. They pushed the poles between their legs and the spikes struck the ice hard and made the sleds skim forwards. The sharp runners and the spikes made a long path of splintered ice behind them.

Some of the sleds had passengers on them, whole families grouped together, with bundles beside them as though they were going on long journeys. Others were loaded with vegetables or rolls of matting or other things to sell. Still others had nothing on them

Their mother watched them go

at all, and Little Pear's father called to the man who was pushing one of these sleds.

"Hi!" he called, and the sled swerved around and came to a sudden stop right beside the bank.

"We should like to go to the city," said Little Pear's father.

So after he and the sled-man had talked to each other for a while about how much money the ride would cost, and everything was settled, all the family got on the sled. They sat down cross-legged on the straw mat that was spread over it, all except Little Pear, who sat at the very front of the sled with his legs stuck out straight in front of him. Then off they sped down the river.

Little Pear sat still for a long time. He was looking at all the other sleds. He looked at the sleds that they passed, and at the sleds that passed them. It was like a race. He looked at the sleds on the other side of the river that were going in the opposite direction, and wondered if there were a great city in that direction too, if you traveled far enough.

"I like going to cities," thought Little Pear.

There were villages every once in a while, built close to the river's edge. At first the villages were far apart, but the nearer their sled drew to the city the closer together the villages were. Finally they were like one long village that had no end. Children

The sled swerved around

ran out of the small dust-colored houses to watch the sleds going by, and Little Pear and Dagu and Ergu waved to them.

There were more sleds than ever on the river now. Little Pear wondered where they had all come from so suddenly. It was hard work for one sled to pass another. Little Pear felt so excited by all the crowd of sleds and by all the sights along the banks that he stood up to see them better.

"Sit down," said his father. "You'll fall over if you're not careful." But Little Pear was so interested in what he was seeing that he didn't hear his father.

A village on the riverbank

He kept on standing up. Then at last he could see the city wall!

"Look, Ergu! Look, Dagu!" he cried. But "Look out!" cried Dagu and Ergu at the same time. For just then their sled struck another sled in front of them. There was a terrific jolt—and Little Pear fell off on the ice!

There was a great deal of shouting then. The two men who were pushing the two sleds were calling out to each other that it was all the other one's fault. Little Pear's father and Dagu and Ergu were crying, "Stop! Stop!" And all the people on all the other sleds were calling out, "Whose fault was it?" "It was that man's fault!" "No, it was the other one's fault!" And meanwhile, there was Little Pear on the ice.

There was a bump on his forehead, and he felt surprised and dazed, and he didn't know at first what had happened. Then all around him he saw sleds, and still more sleds, and he thought that surely he would be run over. He wanted to run away, but he didn't know where to run, and besides, he was so cold and had had such a bad fall that he could hardly have moved if he'd tried. He sat there wondering what was going to happen next. And the sleds circled around him so as not to hurt him. They didn't run over him.

It wasn't really very long before his father reached him and picked him up off the ice, but it seemed like an hour to Little Pear. How glad he was to be safe on the sled once more, with Dagu and Ergu beside him!

"Does your bump hurt much?" asked Ergu.

"Were you very frightened? " asked Dagu.

Little Pear shook his head. "I didn't cry," he said.

And perhaps it was because of that, and perhaps it was because Little Pear had had enough punishment, but anyway, his father didn't scold him for standing up on the sled when he had told him not to. And when they reached the city he bought him

a toy cart with round yellow wheels that played a tune as they turned around, which made the bump on Little Pear's head feel almost well.

But he bought presents for Dagu and Ergu, too, because they were good little girls.

How There Was a Tiger for the New Year

Shing-er's favorite toy was the cloth tiger Big Head had given him when he was one month old. Little Pear liked the tiger too, and played with it sometimes when Shing-er was playing with something else. It was about the size of a kitten, and was striped orange and black. It had a pleasant face, and looked as though it were smiling. Little Pear had never seen a real tiger, and he thought that they all looked like this one. He told Ergu that he was very fond of tigers.

When it was nearly time for the New Year there were all kinds of preparations going on in the house. The New Year is the happiest time of the year in China. Everybody has new clothes then, and especially good things to eat. And for two weeks everybody has a holiday.

Little Pear was very anxious for the New Year to come. There would be all sorts of things to see and do then. There would be firecrackers to set off and skyrockets to watch, and perhaps there would be a conjuror or an acrobat.

While his mother and sisters made fancy cakes and cooked meatballs and other tempting things for the New Year, Little Pear ran errands and minded the baby. He was being very good, and not getting into any mischief because he hoped he would get some new toys for the New Year, as well as new clothes.

One day when Dagu and Ergu were sewing and Shing-er was asleep and Little Pear was playing with the tiger, Ergu said, "There is going to be another tiger in our house at New Year's time."

Little Pear pricked up his ears. "What?" he cried. "Another tiger! Will it be just like this one?"

"Oh, no," said Ergu, smiling. "It's going to be a different kind of tiger. Now go out-of-doors and play, Little Pear. We are very busy here, Dagu and I."

So Little Pear went out-of-doors to look for Big Head. He wanted to tell him about the new tiger that was coming.

He found Big Head walking along the village street, looking important. He had an enormous kettle in his arms almost as big as he. "I am borrowing this for my mother," he said. "She is cooking for the New Year."

Little Pear walked along beside Big Head. "We are going to have a tiger in our house at New Year's time," he said.

Big Head almost dropped his kettle. "A tiger?" he said in surprise. "A live one or a toy?"

"A live one," said Little Pear.

"Will it bite?" asked Big Head.

"Not unless you treat it badly," said Little Pear.

Big Head had stopped feeling surprised. "I don't believe you are going to have a real live tiger at all," he said. "There aren't any around here."

"Will the tiger bite?" asked Big Head

Little Pear didn't know very much about tigers, and he certainly didn't know very much about this one. But he didn't want Big Head to know this. He nodded his head solemnly and said, "You wait and see."

Until the beginning of the New Year, Little Pear could think of nothing but tigers. He wondered if the new tiger would have a smiling face like Shing-er's toy one, and he wondered if it really would bite. When he asked Ergu or Dagu about it they only laughed and looked mysterious, and when he asked his father and mother they only laughed, too. Everybody laughed except Shing-er.

"We are going to have a real live tiger," Little Pear told him. And Shing-er opened his eyes wide and looked around the room as though he knew what his brother was saying and expected to see a tiger right away.

At last the New Year came and the holidays began. Little Pear could tell when they had started because of the firecrackers. "Crack-crack-crack! Crack-crack-crack!"

He heard them when he first opened his eyes in the early morning, and he felt so excited that he slid right out of bed. He put on his new clothes that were lying ready for him, a fine green jacket and purple trousers and black shoes; and he was out of the house and away before the others were even up.

He ran out into the street and he never stopped running until he came to the place where the fire-crackers were being set off. There was a crowd of boys there already, and the man who was setting off the firecrackers was quite surrounded. Little Pear pushed his way through the crowd and watched with the rest. He thought the sound of firecrackers pop-ping was the best sound in the world, and the sight of the red firecrackers almost the finest sight, too.

But before he could beg to light one himself he felt someone tug his arm. It was Big Head.

"Come with me," said Big Head. "There's a conjuror in the next street, and a juggler, and it's even more fun to watch them than to watch firecrackers going off! Come and see them, Little Pear!"

So Little Pear followed Big Head and hurried with him to the next street. There was a still greater crowd here. More people were up and out-of-doors now, and nearly half the village seemed to be here to watch the conjuror and the juggler.

The conjuror was a tall man, with a clever-looking face. He wore a long blue gown over his other clothes. The juggler looked clever, too. He was thinly dressed in just a jacket and trousers, so that he could move quickly.

When Little Pear and Big Head came up it was the juggler who was performing. He was spinning plates on sticks. On each hand was balanced a stick, with a plate spinning on the end of each, and in the air a third plate was spinning! Before this plate could

fall to the ground the juggler caught it on one of the sticks and the plate that had been on that stick before spun in the air instead. It was like magic. None of the three plates ever fell to the ground. At last the juggler caught all the plates on one stick, and the spinning was over. Now it was the conjuror's turn, and everyone crowded nearer.

The conjuror spread a cloth upon the ground. Then he set six little bowls on it, upside down. He lifted each one up in turn, so that people could look

inside and see that each one was empty. And then with a short stick he tapped one on the side.

"Long-dong, long-dong, chi-ba long-dong," he said, and lifted up the bowl. There, underneath it, was a round red berry! It had certainly not been there before.

After everybody had stared at the berry and made sure that it was real, the conjuror covered it up with the same bowl. Once more he said the magic words, but this time he lifted up another bowl. And there was the berry again!

Little Pear and Big Head were watching with their eyes and mouths quite round. This man was certainly a fine conjuror, they thought. "Do something more! Do something more!" they cried. And so the conjuror rolled up his sleeves and thought of other things to do.

He stood in the center of the crowd in his long gown, and the people around him could see him on all sides. Then, "Long-dong, long-dong, chi-ba long-dong," he said, and drew out from under his coat a huge bowl of goldfish, with water splashing over the sides. It seemed as though it couldn't be a real bowl of goldfish since it hadn't been there a moment before. But the water that splashed into the street was real, and so were the goldfish, swimming round and round inside the bowl.

"Long-dong, long-dong, chi-ba long-dong"

"Ay-ah," thought Big Head and Little Pear. "This is more fun than firecrackers!"

They watched the conjuror for a long time. They watched him take a paper fan that was quite smooth and whole, and wave it through the air with a swish—and there it was all in tatters. And they watched him wave it through the air once more, and there it was whole and smooth again!

They watched both the conjuror and the juggler for so long that at last they both began to feel rather queer. "I haven't had anything to eat yet," said Big Head.

"Neither have I," said Little Pear. "I forgot all about breakfast."

They both started off toward home.

Big Head reached his house first, and Little Pear went on alone. He walked along slowly, thinking

There it was whole and smooth again!

about magic things, when all at once he remembered
something else. The tiger! Had it come yet? He was
so excited that he ran, but when he was almost home
he stopped and wondered. What if the tiger really
should bite?

"I am not afraid of tigers anyway," he decided.
So he turned the corner and came in sight of his
own gateway. And the nearer he came to it the more
puzzled he was, and when he was *quite* near he
laughed out loud. "Is that our tiger?" he cried.

For there on the doorstep was Ergu, all dressed up in her best New Year's clothes with a red coat on and a pink flower in her hair: and there on Ergu's lap was Shing-er, who was dressed in his New Year's clothes, too.

His coat was of orange and black cloth, striped like a tiger. His cap was like a tiger's head, with little furry ears. Even his shoes were like two tigers, with green glass eyes on the toes.

How Little Pear laughed! And Ergu laughed, too. "He *is* alive," said Little Pear.

"But he doesn't bite," said Ergu.

Shing-er didn't say anything but he looked proud and pleased with his fine new clothes.

"I think this is a very good tiger we have," said Little Pear; and he admiringly stroked the furry ears on Shing-er's cap.

7

How Little Pear Took His Bird
for a Walk

All through the New Year's festival there were feasts during the day and fireworks at night. For two whole weeks the holiday lasted, but those two weeks seemed to pass very quickly, and when they were over it was nearly spring and the ice had melted on the pond and on the river.

On windy days the village children flew their kites that they had been given at New Year's, but on days when there was no wind there was not so much to do.

On one of these days Little Pear was walking along down the street, wondering what to do, when he suddenly remembered that he had six pennies in the pocket that was inside his coat. They were pennies that had been given to him for New Year's and he had been doing so many other things that he had forgotten to spend them. He decided to go and buy something with them right away.

But while he was walking toward the street where the shops were he met a man who was carrying a birdcage. There was a bird in the cage, hopping about on his perch and looking very happy. He looked at Little Pear with his bright eyes, and cocked his head at him.

Little Pear trotted along beside the man with the bird. "Do you like birds, too?" asked the man.

"Yes," said Little Pear. "I have one at home."

"I am taking my bird for a walk," said the man. "He likes to go for a walk now and then and take a look at everything."

Little Pear said good-bye to the man and hurried off toward home. He had had a sudden idea. He would take his own bird for a walk!

He met a man who was carrying a birdcage

This bird lived in a cage that hung by the door in Little Pear's house. Once Little Pear had opened the door of the cage and let the bird fly away into the sky like the other birds who were free. It had come back after a long time but Little Pear had been told that he must never let it fly away again. Still, he often felt sorry for it. He knew if he were kept shut up in a cage he would like to see the world sometimes.

So he thought that it would be a good idea to take his bird for a walk. It would be almost as much fun for him as flying away.

Nobody was at home when he went into his house except the bird, who was looking rather lonely. Little Pear climbed on a bench so that he could reach its cage. "Would you like to go for a walk?" he asked, and, "cheep, cheep!" answered the bird, fluttering its wings.

So very carefully Little Pear climbed down from the bench with the birdcage in his hands. Then he carried it out into the sunny courtyard. "See," he said to the bird. "I am going to take you for a long walk, out through the front gate. You are going to see the whole village!"

The bird said, "cheep," again and hopped about. And Little Pear went out through the gate and down the street, swinging the cage gently to and fro.

He climbed down from the bench very carefully

Some of his friends were playing tag in the street,
Big Head and his brother Didi and a few others.
They stopped their game when they saw Little Pear
coming along carrying a birdcage.

"What are you doing?" they called, and Little
Pear answered, "I am taking my bird for a walk!"

His friends came crowding around him to look
at the bird. "Let me hold the cage for a while," said
one. "No, let me!" said another.

So Little Pear said, "You may take turns carrying it. But when I want it again myself you must let me have it."

His friends agreed, so first one and then another took a turn at carrying the birdcage. The bird was having a lovely time.

But all at once there came a cry from farther down the street. "Tang-hulurs! Tang-hulurs!" a voice was calling. Little Pear forgot to watch the bird a little anxiously as it was handed from one boy to another. He was remembering the six pennies that he hadn't spent yet. He knew now what he wanted to do with them. Tang-hulurs were his favorite kind of candy.

Before the tang-hulur man came in sight Little Pear knew just what the tang-hulurs would look like. Candied red berries on sticks, all frozen over with hard syrup. He knew what they would taste like, too: sweet and sour, crisp and sticky, all at the same time. He felt in his inside pocket and there were the pennies, with holes in the middle, tied safely on a string. And then he ran to meet the tang-hulur man as he came in sight down toward the end of the street.

"Tang-hulurs! Tang-hulurs!" the man kept crying. A tray of tang-hulurs was swung in front of him and in his hand was a great fan-shaped bunch of them.

His friends came crowding around to look at the bird

"How much are they?" asked Little Pear. "Two pennies a stick," said the man. Little Pear thought hard. Two pennies for one, four pennies for two, six pennies for three—He had six pennies, so he could buy three tang-hulurs! One for Dagu, one for Ergu, and one for himself. Shing-er was too young to eat tang-hulurs.

"Three tang-hulurs," he said to the man, and in

exchange for his six pennies he was handed three
sticks of the delicious candy. Then he started toward
home to see if he could find his sisters, and as he
went he began eating the tang-hulur that was for
himself.

But before he reached home his friends crowded
around him once more. "Little Pear," they said,
"what has become of your bird?"

"My bird?" said Little Pear in surprise. He had

forgotten about it for a moment. "Why, you have him!" he cried. "Where is he?"

Nobody seemed to know. Everyone said that it was somebody else who had had the birdcage last. "We'll help you find him, though," they said to Little Pear.

Little Pear was so distressed that he didn't know what to do. He didn't feel a bit hungry anymore. Where was his poor bird? And what if somebody had stolen him and would never give him back?

"I'll give a whole tang-hulur to whoever finds him first," he said.

All the children scattered through the village, looking for the bird. High and low they looked, in houses and in courtyards, in shops and along streets. But there was no sign of either a bird or a birdcage. "Oh, dear, oh, dear," thought Little Pear. "What shall I do?"

At last, when he had almost given up hope of ever seeing the bird again and was slowly dragging his feet toward home, Big Head came running up to him.

"It's at my house!" he cried. "My little brother took it home with him. He didn't know any better."

Little Pear ran to Big Head's house as fast as his legs could carry him. There, sure enough, was

his yellow bird, quite happy and contented, and there was Didi holding tightly to the cage with both hands.

Little Pear remembered his promise. He gave one of his tang-hulurs to Big Head because he had found the bird. But he gave another one to Didi who cried when he took the bird away from him. So when he took his bird home again he only had one tang-hulur left and that was partly gone!

He shared it with Dagu and Ergu who were at home now, and who had been wondering what had become of the bird. And they were all so glad that

the bird hadn't really been lost that they didn't mind
not having a whole stick of candy apiece. After all,
the bird was nicer than a whole trayful of tang-
hulurs.

8

How Big Head Wanted to Look like a Man

Shing-er was getting quite big now. His head had been shaved all except for a round spot of hair above his forehead just like Little Pear's, and like Little Pear he had a tiny pigtail that stood up in the air. They looked very much alike.

Big Head, too, had a shaved head, but he looked different because he had three spots of hair braided into three pigtails. His mother thought this looked very pretty, but Big Head sometimes wished he had only one pigtail like Little Pear, or none at all, like a man.

One day Little Pear was playing out-of-doors with some of his friends. They were playing in the street because the courtyards were rather small, and,

besides, the streets were a good safe place to play in. Very few carts or rickshaws came through the village. Once in a while a man selling something or a traveling tinker would go by, and sometimes there would be a stray pig walking along or a few chickens. But most of the time the streets were quiet and undisturbed, except for the children.

One little boy was spinning a diabolo. It was like a great wooden spool. The little boy held a stick in each hand with a string between them, and he spun the diabolo on the string until it made a humming sound. Little Pear watched him. He watched him spin the diabolo and toss it into the air to catch

it again. It was a lovely kind of plaything, Little Pear thought.

Another boy was playing a game with a shuttle-cock. The shuttlecock was made with three cocks' feathers weighted with two pennies wrapped in a piece of cloth. The boy kicked the shuttlecock into the air with his foot and then before it could fall to the ground, he kicked it again into the air. Over and over again he did this until he had counted twenty-five kicks.

"Ay-ah, that is a very exciting game," Little Pear

thought. He wished that he had a shuttlecock and he thought that if he had one he might be able to kick it thirty times without once letting it fall.

"Let's play leapfrog," somebody suggested, and Little Pear was just going to join in a game of leapfrog when he heard Big Head calling to him. Big Head was looking very important, with his three pigtails tied with three colors of string. He was holding something in his hand.

"Little Pear!" he cried. "Look, I found a ten-

cent piece lying in the street. I am going to the toy shop to spend it right away. Do you want to come, too?"

"Oh, yes!" said Little Pear. He decided that he would much rather go to the toy shop than play leap-frog. So together he and Big Head went off down the street.

Big Head kept talking about all the different kinds of toys that he might buy. There were lots of things in the toy shop that could be bought with a ten-cent piece, he said.

"A diabolo?" asked Little Pear.

"Perhaps," said Big Head.

"Or a shuttlecock?" asked Little Pear.

"Perhaps," said Big Head. "We'll see when we get there."

The toy shop was the most interesting place in the whole village. Nearly always there were children straying in and out of it, looking at all the toys with bright black eyes. Sometimes they had money to spend, and sometimes they just came to look. Little Pear usually just went to look, but it was more fun to buy something, of course. It was fun to help somebody else buy something, too.

There were many things on the way to the toy shop to see and admire. There were the tinware shop and the basket shop and several food shops.

Sniffing the delicious smell

Little Pear and Big Head stopped a minute to watch a man place some steaming loaves of bread upon a tray and to sniff the delicious smell of cabbages cooking. They watched noodles being ladled out of a pot and saw bread being twisted into different shapes. They began to feel rather hungry, but they went on toward the toy shop.

Just before they reached it they nearly bumped into a barber who was setting up his stand in the street.

"Who wants a shave! Who wants a shave!" He was calling out in a sing-song voice. And while he was calling he arranged his stool and his bench and all the shaving things. There was hot water, and there were soap and towels and shining razors. It was fun to watch him getting ready.

"Who wants a shave!" he called, and suddenly Big Head said, "I do!"

The barber laughed out loud. "It would be a pity to shave off those three fine pigtails," he said.

"No," said Big Head. "I am tired of them. I want my head to be shaved all over, like a man."

Little Pear tugged at Big Head's sleeve. "Aren't you going to buy a toy?" he asked anxiously.

"Yes," said Big Head. "But first I want my head shaved."

So Big Head climbed up on the barber's high

Big Head held very still

stool and held very still. And the barber polished his razor and shaved off one, then two, and then the last pigtail. And when he had finished there was Big Head with his head quite round and smooth and no hair anywhere.

"Do I look like a man now?" he asked Little Pear, who had been just as still as Big Head.

"Yes," said Little Pear rather sadly. "But you don't look like Big Head anymore."

Big Head slid down from the stool. "Let's go to the toy shop now," he said.

But, "Wait," said the barber. "You must pay for having your head shaved."

Big Head had forgotten all about that. "How much?" he asked the barber.

"Ten cents."

Big Head and Little Pear looked at each other. That was all the money Big Head had. There could be no toys now. However, it was too late for Big Head to change his mind. His head had already been shaved, and the barber must be paid. So he gave him his precious ten-cent piece.

"I can't buy any toy now," he said.

"Never mind," said the barber. "You can buy a toy another day. Today you have had your head shaved."

"Yes," agreed Big Head quite happily. He was

Placing a bowl of dumplings on the table

very proud of his shaved head. Little Pear, though, felt rather sorrowful. He wished that Big Head had bought a toy instead. A diabolo, perhaps—or a shuttlecock.

When Little Pear went home that evening he found his mother placing a bowl of steamed dumplings on the table, and he was so hungry that he forgot to feel disappointed. But when Big Head went home his mother cried to see his pigtails gone, and said, "You must go without your supper tonight, you are such a bad boy."

But although Big Head was hungry, too, he didn't feel sorry that his head was shaved as smoothly as a ball. He liked it that way.

9

Little Pear Decides to Be a Beggar

It was a lovely day in the early summer and Little Pear was looking for crickets in the grass beside the highroad. He had a box to put them in, a round box made out of a gourd. It had carvings on it, and was stained bright orange. Little Pear thought that the crickets would not mind being caught if they were put in such a pretty box.

The peach trees along the highroad had bloomed and the blossoms had all been blown away by the spring winds. Now the trees were covered with leaves and made cool shadows to play in.

Vegetables were growing in the fields between the highroad and the village. Little Pear's father was working in the fields and his mother was working at home. His sisters were playing with some friends and Shing-er was sitting in the courtyard listening to the bird chirping in his cage. But Little Pear had wanted to look for crickets, so here he was beside the highroad.

Little Pear hummed a tune as he searched about in the grass. He was thinking how happy his family would be if he should bring even one cricket home. Dagu and Ergu liked crickets, he knew, and as for Shing-er, he had never even seen one!

"Perhaps he will say something when he hears it singing inside the box," thought Little Pear. For he was always trying to think of ways to make his brother talk.

Shing-er could crawl a short distance but he couldn't walk or talk yet. Little Pear was afraid sometimes that he was never going to. He kept forgetting that Shing-er was not a year old yet, although ever since the New Year he had been called two years old because he had lived in two different years.

Little Pear hunted and hunted for crickets. But perhaps the crickets had heard him coming and had hidden because they didn't want to be caught, or perhaps some other boys had already caught them all. Whichever it was, he couldn't seem to find any.

Little Pear felt sorry. He wanted so much to take one home to Shing-er, and, besides, it was a pity not to have anything to put in the box. But still, he wasn't sorry that he had come to the highroad. He decided to climb a tree.

So up the nearest tree he went, up and up, holding tightly with his knees and hands. It was hard work. The farther he climbed, the higher the tree seemed to grow. He went up inch by inch, sometimes sliding back a little way. But at last he could reach out his arm and catch hold of the lowest branch. The rest was easy. Up went one leg, up went the other, and there was Little Pear in the tree.

It was lovely up there. There were no blossoms to look at now, and no peaches to eat, but he could look out between the leaves and see the whole countryside. There was his own village, looking quite small and unimportant, with its dust-colored houses and roofs of gray tile or straw. And there was the river with boats sailing down it, far away in the distance.

And there, most interesting of all, was the highroad right below. Little Pear looked down at the carts creaking along, and the wheelbarrows loaded with vegetables, and the travelers walking past with bundles in their hands. It was fun to look at things without being seen.

There was always an endless procession of carts and people going to the city. Little Pear wished that he might join the procession, but he had promised his family never to run away again, after the time when he had fallen into the river. So he just watched rather sadly from his tree.

There was the highroad right below

But suddenly he remembered the beggar boys he had seen running along the highroad once. At the same time he remembered the box which he had left under the tree when he had started to climb.

"I will be a beggar," thought Little Pear. He had never promised not to be a beggar; and that was not at all the same thing as running away.

Down he slid from the tree, and although in his hurry he tore a hole in his jacket, he didn't think that mattered. The more holes the better, for a beggar.

He picked up his box. It would be a very good thing to put pennies in. Then he drew a deep breath. And then he started running along the highroad.

Beside the carts and rickshaws he ran, holding out his hand. But he felt too shy to say, "Give me

some money! Give me some money!" because he had never been a beggar boy before.

The people in the carts and rickshaws seemed to know what he expected, though. Some of them, who might have been too poor or too proud, didn't give him anything at all: but others who might have had more money than they knew what to do with, or else just liked to give money to beggars, threw pennies to him. Some of them he caught, but most of them he had to pick up from the ground.

At first Little Pear thought it was quite easy being a beggar. All he had to do was to run along and hold out his hand.

But after a while he thought it was rather hard. How fast he had to run to keep up with the rickshaws! And even the slow lumbering carts moved

faster than he could run, because his legs were so
short.

When somebody threw him money that he couldn't
catch he had to pick it up quickly before a rickshaw-
puller shouted to him to get out of the way. And he
had to dodge out from under horses' hoofs and mind
the hind legs of briskly trotting donkeys.

Little Pear really looked like a beggar now, he
was so covered with dust. His face was as dusty as
his hands, and his clothes were powdered with a
layer of dust. The strips of cloth that tied his trousers
down neatly around his ankles had come unwound
and nearly tripped him up.

"Ay-ah!" thought Little Pear, after he had run
and dodged and picked up pennies for a long time.
"I am tired of being a beggar!"

He stopped at the edge of the highroad, where
he was in nobody's way, to count his pennies.

"Two—four—six—eleven—" What a lot of
pennies there were! He put them safely in his box,
where they made a pleasant jingling sound. He felt
very rich.

But he also felt very tired. When he looked back
along the way he had come it seemed as though he
could never run or even walk that distance. There
was the long highroad as far as he could see and
the line of trees on either side of it met in a point
at the end.

The trees met in a point

"How far I have come!" thought Little Pear.

But he looked in the other direction and there not very far ahead was a village, the first of the villages that the highroad passed through before it reached the city. And Little Pear was so hot and thirsty that he thought he would go on to that village and get a cup of tea to drink before he turned back toward home.

"I can buy some tea with one of my pennies," he thought.

So on he went, not begging now, and before long he reached the village.

The highroad was a street now. Shops opened on the street, and one of the first ones was a food shop. Little Pear stopped at it.

"May I have a cup of tea?" he asked. The shopman looked at him in great surprise. "You look as though you had been on a long journey," he said.

Little Pear nodded his head. "I am on my way home now," he said; and then, as the shopman still stared at him, he took a penny out of his box and handed it to him.

"I'm very thirsty," he said.

The shopman didn't say anything more, but he poured out a cup of tea for him. And then, when Little Pear had drunk it all, he said, "You had better

"May I have a cup of tea?"

hurry home, now. Your mother will be wondering where you are."

"Oh, no," said Little Pear. "I'm a big boy." But he felt a little anxious just the same.

He turned to go home, when another shop right opposite caught his eye. It seemed to be a clothes shop, but what interested Little Pear was a row of hats hanging up outside. They were straw hats with round turned-up brims, and they were trimmed with fancy pink and green pompons. Little Pear thought, "What pretty hats," and then he thought, "They are meant for a small child," and *then* he thought, "Perhaps I could buy one for Shing-er."

"Don't spend all your money," said the shop-

A row of hats

man's voice behind him, but Little Pear didn't pay any attention to him. He hurried across the street to where the hats were.

Another shopman met him there. "How much?" asked Little Pear, pointing to the hats. This shopman also stared at him. "They are very fine hats," he said. "I am afraid they are too expensive for you to buy."

"I have ten pennies," said Little Pear, holding out his box.

The shopman looked at his anxious face and at his dusty clothes, and smiled. "Very well," he said. "They are really more than that, but I will let you have one for ten pennies."

So Little Pear emptied the box into the shopman's hand and took the smallest hat there was. It looked as though it would just exactly fit Shing-er.

Then he started for home, feeling so happy that he forgot about being tired.

And as he walked along the hot dusty highroad he held the straw hat very tightly and carefully, thinking how pleased Shing-er would be when he saw it.

On and on walked Little Pear, keeping to the side of the highroad so that he should not be bumped into. The sun was high and the day grew hotter and

It looked as though it would just fit Shing-er

more dusty, but Little Pear was so dusty already that more dust didn't matter very much.

He was not a beggar anymore. It was far too hot to run after the carts and rickshaws. It was almost too hot to walk, but Little Pear kept on and on, because he had been away from home so long and he was afraid his family might think that he had run away.

Little Pear wished that he might ask for a ride in a cart. But the carts he saw were all going in the wrong direction. He wished that he might ask for a ride in a rickshaw. But the rickshaws all had people in them already. So on and on went Little Pear, on his two feet, until a jingling sound behind him made him turn his head. There was a man riding on a donkey, and it was the bells around the donkey's neck that jingled. The man called out to Little Pear, "Would you like a ride?"

"Oh, yes!" cried Little Pear. In a minute the man had jumped to the ground and lifted Little Pear, hat and box and all, onto the donkey's back. Then he got on himself, behind him, and away they rode!

Little Pear had never ridden on a donkey before. He was so excited that he couldn't say anything. But when the donkey began to gallop, he laughed out loud. They passed all the carts and all the rickshaws and all the men with bundles. They went faster than anything else on the highroad.

Almost in no time Little Pear saw his village, looking just the same as when he had left it. He was glad to see it again, but sorry that his ride was over. "That is where I live," he told the man on the donkey.

The man set him down on the ground. "Were you afraid?" he asked him.

"Oh, no," said Little Pear. "I like to ride on donkeys!"

The man touched the donkey with his whip and off they trotted down the road. And Little Pear watched

Away they rode!

them for a while and then went across the fields towards his village. Soon he had reached his home.

"Oh, Little Pear!" cried his mother when she saw him. "Where have you been?" Then, before he could answer, she cried, "What have you done to your clothes? You look like a beggar boy!"

Little Pear looked down at his dusty clothes. "I'm not a beggar anymore!" he said.

Then he told her of his adventures on the highroad and showed her the hat he had bought for Shing-er.

"It's very pretty," said his mother. "But being a beggar is just as bad as running away." And, while she washed his face and hands and put a clean jacket on him, she made Little Pear promise never, never to be a beggar boy again.

But she didn't spank him.

1 0

Little Pear Takes Care of Shing-er

Little Pear wanted to give Shing-er his present right away. "Where is he?" he asked his mother, as soon as he was washed and had a clean jacket on.

"He is playing in the courtyard," she said.

Little Pear shook his head. "I didn't see him."

His mother ran to the door and looked out. There was the courtyard, quite bare except for the toy tiger

His mother ran to the door

and an empty wheelbarrow. Shing-er was nowhere in sight.

"Dagu or Ergu must have taken him out into the street," said Little Pear's mother. But she looked rather worried, and hurried across to the gateway.

"Dagu! Ergu!" she called.

Little Pear followed her.

"Dagu! Ergu!" cried his mother again, and soon the two girls came running around the corner.

"Is it suppertime already?" they said. Neither one of them was carrying Shing-er.

"Where is Shing-er?" said their mother. "Wasn't he with you?"

"No," said Dagu and Ergu together. "We thought he was playing in the courtyard."

"He isn't here," said their mother, "but he was here just a little while ago. Are you sure you didn't take him out into the street?"

But Dagu and Ergu shook their heads. They hadn't taken Shing-er with them.

"Oh, dear!" cried Little Pear. "He must have run away!"

His mother and sisters said, No, that couldn't be. Shing-er couldn't walk. He must have been stolen.

"Go into the field and tell your father, Little Pear," said his mother. "And, Dagu and Ergu, help

me look for him in the village. Perhaps the neighbors have seen him."

Little Pear ran off as fast as he could go. Down the path he went, forgetting that he had ever been tired of running. They must find Shing-er!

He was quite out of breath when he reached his

father, who was working in his cabbage field— "Sh-Sh-Shing-er is lost!" he panted.

His father wouldn't believe him at first. "He can't be," he said.

"Ye-ye-yes, he is!" said Little Pear, nodding his head very hard.

His father believed him this time, and stopped his work. He started off for the village with such long steps that Little Pear could hardly keep up with him. When they reached the village nearly everybody there seemed to know of the disappearance of Shing-er. Everybody was searching, looking in houses, and asking each other questions, and peeping into every wheelbarrow.

Supper was forgotten, and the fields were forgotten. Men and women and children were all looking for Shing-er.

Little Pear felt sadder even than when he had thought his bird was lost. But the bird had been found, so maybe Shing-er would be found, too.

"Are you sure you haven't seen him?" he asked Big Head's little brother. But Didi hadn't seen him, and neither had Big Head. They were looking for him too.

The sun was low now, and soon it would be dark. Little Pear had been lost once in the dark and he hadn't liked it at all. Dogs had barked, and he

"Are you sure you haven't seen him?"

had almost been afraid of them. He must find poor Shing-er!

Everybody else was searching in the village. Nobody was looking in the fields. Little Pear ran down into the fields by himself, past the pond where he had skated in the winter and where frogs were singing now, and then he stopped to think. He decided to walk all the way around the village, in a circle along the edge of the fields.

He didn't have to go very far. When he came to the edge of the field that was nearest his own house he saw Shing-er lying fast asleep in the tall grass. He had crawled there all by himself.

"Father! Mother! Dagu! Ergu!" called Little Pear.

In a little while there was a crowd around Little Pear and Shing-er. And in a still shorter time they were both at home again, surrounded by all the family and as many of the neighbors as the house could hold.

Everyone was talking at once, but Little Pear talked the loudest. *"He must have walked there!"* he said. And then he remembered something. He ran and got the straw hat with pink and green pompons and held it out to Shing-er who was quite wide awake now and seemed to be enjoying all the crowd and the excitement.

And when Shing-er saw the hat he stretched his hands out to it. "Hat!" he said.

Dagu, Ergu, and Little Pear looked at each other in delight. "Shing-er can walk and talk now!" they said.

Everybody felt very happy. They admired Shing-

er in his new hat, and they praised Little Pear for having found his brother.

"You really can take care of him," said his mother.

"And he needs to be taken care of every minute," said Ergu very solemnly. "Because I'm afraid he's going to be just as mischievous as Little Pear!"

Eleanor Frances Lattimore (1904–1986) was an American citizen born and raised in Shanghai. She began her career as an artist, but became known as the author and illustrator of more than fifty popular children's books. A number of her stories are based on her experiences growing up in China.